The BEST GINGERBREAD RACE Ever!

by Kelly Hargrave
Illustrated by John Joven

SCHOLASTIC INC.

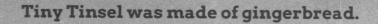

Tiny Tinsel was made of gingerbread.

He was a little spicy,

a lot sweet,

extra shiny,

and super de-duper tiny!
But being small didn't hold him back
from his favorite day of all . . .

Good luck finding a way around that fluffy fur!

Sprinkle Toes

She leaves a trail of sprinkles wherever she goes!

Cotton Candy Yeti

Lucky Licorice

His long legs leap unbelievable lengths!

Bubblegum Beary

Those bubblegum paws bounce him high into the sky!

Giggling Gumdrop

Her wand fires gumdrops when she giggles!

Tiny Tinsel

Down here!

He may be tiny, but his heart is mighty!

Tiny Tinsel knew he was the underdog, but he'd dreamed of running in the Great Gingerbread Race ever since his first day out of the oven.

He practiced running laps around his hot chocolate pond and leaping over stacks of marshmallows.

Now it was finally his time to shine!

With the toot of a lollipop whistle, the racers were off!

Tiny Tinsel was already far behind, but he didn't let that get him down.

He ran, skipped, and hopped, until he noticed something odd up ahead.

Sprinkle Toes and Cotton Candy Yeti
were stuck together and surrounded
by a sea of sprinkles!

"Oh my frosting, what happened here?"
asked Tiny Tinsel.

"Cotton Candy Yeti tripped on my sprinkles and landed right on top of me!" said Sprinkle Toes.

This was the perfect time for Tiny Tinsel to get ahead, but he looked down at his big shiny heart and . . .

His tiny feet were perfect for tiptoeing around sprinkles
without slipping! Then he pulled Sprinkle Toes free.

Using his shimmery icing, he made her a pair of shoes to
keep her sprinkles from spilling . . . and Yeti from falling!

Then they all raced off together, until . . .

Tiny Tinsel's hands were perfect for undoing even tinier knots!

Cotton Candy Yeti stuffed big tufts
of blue fluff in Giggling Gumdrop's ears.

I can't hear any more jokes!

Then they all raced off together, until . . .

It was none other than Bubblegum Beary stuck in a peppermint tree!
"Oh my frosting, what happened here?" asked Tiny Tinsel.

"I bounced so high
I landed in this tree
and now I'm stuck!"

This was the perfect time for Tiny Tinsel to get ahead,
but he looked down at his big shiny heart and . . .

Tiny Tinsel was light enough
to be easily lifted to the top of the tree.

Then he ninja-chopped Bubblegum Beary free!

"Hooray! I get to bounce another day!"

Then they all raced off together, until . . .

They came across a raging root beer river
with the finish line just on the other side.

"What on eggnog's earth are we to do?"
asked Sprinkle Toes.

But Tiny Tinsel already knew!

They tied one end of a long
piece of licorice to a donut tree.

Then Bubblegum Beary
bounced across the river . . .

He tied the other end to a tall lollipop.

Then with a hoot and a holler,
the others quickly followed!

"But that wasn't just me," said Tiny Tinsel, "that was a whole lot of WE!
I've got one more idea, something the crowd will never expect."

They crossed the finish line together.

You're ALL winners!

The announcer cheered. It was the best gingerbread race ever!

Thanks to Tiny Tinsel's big heart.

ISBN 978-1-338-58193-5

10 9   22 23

Printed in the U.S.A.   40

First printing 2019

Book design by Jennifer Rinaldi
Illustrated by John Joven

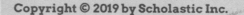